There's a grandad in my soup

Hilary Hawkes

Illustrations by David Mostyn

Scripture Union

By the same author – for younger readers
1, 2, 5 Go!

Copyright © Hilary Hawkes 2002
First published 2002

Scripture Union, 207–209 Queensway, Bletchley,
Milton Keynes, MK2 2EB, England.
Email: info@scriptureunion.org.uk
Web site: www.scriptureunion.org.uk

ISBN 1 85999 414 8

British Library Cataloguing-in-Publication Data.
A catalogue record of this book is available from the British
Library.

Printed and bound in Great Britain by Creative Print and
Design (Wales) Ebbw Vale.

Scripture Union is an international Christian charity working
with churches in more than 130 countries, providing
resources to bring the good news about Jesus Christ to
children, young people and families and to encourage them
to develop spiritually through the Bible and prayer.

As well as our network of volunteers, staff and associates
who run holidays, church-based events and school Christian
groups, we produce a wide range of publications and support
those who use our resources through training programmes.

Chapter One

It was impossible. Danny couldn't believe it. He sat up in bed and looked at his alarm clock.

"Half-past seven. That's amazing!"

Danny threw back the covers and jumped out of bed. He thumped the switch on the top of his clock. Never in his whole life had Danny managed to wake up on a school day before his alarm went off.

It wasn't that Danny stayed up late playing computer games. Certainly not. It wasn't that he spent hours every night doing his homework. Definitely not. No. The reason why Danny usually overslept was THE SNORING.

Danny's dad, super chef, cookery expert, inventor of all mouth-watering delights and boss of The Cuckoo Lane Restaurant, was also the world's loudest snorer. He kept everyone awake: Danny's mum, older sister Lily and Grandad. Danny was usually woken up several times each night by his Dad's snortling pig noises. But last night, Danny's mum had had a brilliant idea. She had given him her spare pair of earplugs. Danny had slept all night without one single snortling pig sound disturbing him.

He couldn't wait to tell Mum they had worked.

Danny crashed down the corridor towards the kitchen. Grandad was sitting at the kitchen table reading yesterday's newspaper. Lily was having a fight with the ironing board.

"Where's Mum?" Danny said.

Grandad jumped from behind his paper.

"Oh, good morning, Danny. No need to

shout. Mum's gone out early to get the shopping."

"Is Mum up yet?" Danny said again.

Lily was shaking the ironing board.

"She's out," she said.

"Pardon?" said Danny.

Grandad looked at Lily. Lily looked at Grandad.

"What's the matter with your hearing this morning, Danny?" she said.

Danny went over to a cupboard and started clattering about with the breakfast bowls.

"Careful," said Lily. "You'll break one of those in a minute. Mind that—"

Crash! Danny caught the biscuit tin with his elbow. It landed on the floor. Danny didn't appear to notice.

"Is Mum still in bed?" he asked, settling himself down at the breakfast table. No answer.

"Why isn't anyone talking to me?" said Danny.

"I think there's something wrong with his

ears," said Lily.

Grandad put the newspaper down and looked very seriously at Danny.

"Only the right one," he said. "He's always had odd ears. Don't you remember? When he was a baby your mum used to put sticky tape over his right ear to stop it sticking out."

"What are you whispering about?" said Danny.

"No," said Lily. "I mean, I can see something sticking out of his ears, and it's not wax."

Grandad and Lily both peered at Danny's ears. Grandad laughed.

"You're right," he said. "Danny's left some earplugs in."

"What?" said Danny.

"There's something in your ears," said Lily. "Take them out!"

"What?" said Danny.

Lily pointed at her ears.

"EARPLUGS!" she shouted.

"You've got earplugs?" said Danny.

"NO! You have! TAKE THEM OUT!"
Take them out? Earplugs?

"Oh!" Danny remembered. He'd forgotten to remove them! He pulled the earplugs out quickly. Sound flooded his head.

Grandad howled with laughter and Danny started to feel daft.

"I put them in last night," he explained.

"Dad's snoring was terrible."

Lily went back to her ironing.

"Maybe you could invent something to stop him snoring, Grandad," she said.

Grandad slotted some sliced bread into the Automatic Breakfast Server. The Automatic Breakfast Server was just one of Grandad's many inventions. Grandad might be seventy-five years old but his inventions, which had earned him a living for many years, were still going strong. Sometimes Grandad managed to invent quite useful things. There was the time he'd designed a supermarket trolley with brakes and gears. His electric window washers were still selling like hot cakes.

Since Grandad had come to live with Danny and his family in the flat above the restaurant, he did most of his inventing in the garage. He had turned it into a workshop. No one was allowed in Grandad's workshop while he was working on things because he liked them to be a surprise. He had been busy on his latest idea for about two months now.

Ping!

The warning bell on the Automatic Breakfast Server sent Grandad and Danny rushing to put four plates in position on the kitchen table.

Zoom! The first slice of toast shot out and

landed on the floor. The second followed and landed in the sink. The third landed on the ironing board which Lily had just managed to get into a standing position and the fourth...

"Ow!"

...shot across the room and wopped Dad in the face as he entered the kitchen.

"I just don't understand what's gone wrong with that machine," said Grandad. "It was working perfectly last week. They're supposed to land on the plates."

"I'll help you fix it," said Danny, hoping this might get him entry to the workshop and a look at Grandad's new invention.

"I'll tell you what does need fixing," said Lily, speed-ironing her jeans, "and that's your hair, Dad."

It was true. Ever since Dad had accidentally washed his hair in Mum's hair dye instead of shampoo a week ago he had been walking around like a carrot.

"Funny how it went orange when it said brown on the bottle," Lily frowned.

"Very odd indeed," said Dad, who seemed strangely unbothered by the accident. "But at least now your mother and I are a matching pair."

This, unfortunately, was also true. Danny cringed at the thought of his parents turning up at Parents' Evening or Sports Day with their matching orange hair. Thank goodness there wasn't anything on for parents to turn up to at the moment. Then he had a horrible thought.

"The restaurant inspectors are coming in two days!" he said. "I don't suppose, I mean, I don't suppose it will have washed out by then?"

"Well, I hope not," said Dad. He was taking milk and eggs and bacon out of the fridge. "We'll have to get another bottle of it."

In no time at all Dad had cooked one of his best omelettes. With a super chef in the house, who needs an Automatic Breakfast Server? Danny thought, tucking in.

Ten minutes later Dad and Lily went down

to the restaurant. It might be only quarter-past eight but there were tables to be set, menus to be sorted, tablecloths to be taken to the launderette and vegetables to be put away when Mum got back with them.

Danny went off to get dressed. A few minutes later he was back in the kitchen. His hair was tousled, his shirt was hanging out and his tie was crooked; in other words, he was ready for school.

Grandad was getting the Automatic Breakfast Server ready to take down to his workshop. It might be a mad idea but Danny knew Grandad would get it working. He always got things working. It was what he was good at. Danny stuffed his homework into his book bag. It seemed to Danny that everyone in his family was good at something. Mum had the restaurant running like clockwork and Lily, who was seventeen now, was the best waitress ever. Only the other day she had managed to carry five dinner plates, two jugs of gravy and a large cherry cheesecake all at the same time. If *he* tried that... well, it didn't bear thinking about.

Danny knew that God made everyone different and that everyone had something they were good at. Except it didn't make sense. Surely there wasn't anything *he* was good at? He stuffed his sketch book into his rucksack with his lunch box.

"See you later then," said Grandad. "All the best with the spelling test."

Danny groaned. Spelling – definitely *not* something he was good at.

They walked down the stairs to the back yard together.

"Tell you what," said Grandad, "after school you can be the first to see my next invention. How about that?"

"Wow!" Danny couldn't believe it. "Brilliant! Thanks, Grandad!"

He couldn't wait. Somehow Danny just knew that Grandad's next invention was going to be something fantastic! How was he going to get through a whole day at school before he found out?

Chapter Two

"And now get your spelling books out please, Year Four!"

Danny had been dreading those words all day. Miss May had left the test until ten to three. The whole day had been torture. The whole class had been in torture. Apart from Robert Belch, of course. Robert Belch always got his spellings right.

Robert sat next to Danny.

"Good luck," he whispered.

"Hmm!" said Danny. He needed more than luck. He needed a brain like Robert's.

Danny quickly prayed. "Help me to remember all the words!"

"The first word," Miss May said, "is MISSISSIPPI."

Mrs What? It wasn't fair. Danny couldn't remember any words like that in the list.

"It's a surprise word!" said Miss May. "Write it down everyone!"

It was a surprise all right. A nasty surprise. Robert was the only one writing. The next six words were better. But then came a hard one, almost as bad as Mississippi. It had been on the list, but Danny just *couldn't* remember how it went.

COMPUTER. Was that 'er' at the end or 'or'?

He pushed his spelling book aside. His sketch pad was underneath, open at a fresh page. Danny started doodling. Sometimes if he doodled it helped him remember things. Danny drew a picture of a computer. It was very good.

"Finish that last word and put your pencils down," said Miss May.

Suddenly Danny remembered: it was 'er'. It was definitely 'er'. He wrote it quickly and put his pencil down. Phew! It was over. It was home time at last. Danny felt a ripple of excitement as he remembered Grandad's invention. Miss May was collecting the spelling books and telling everyone to fetch their coats.

"Don't forget the extra day off school on Thursday," she was saying.

No one had forgotten. The teachers were going on a special course. It would be the same day as the restaurant inspectors' visit.

Danny was about to make a dash for the door.

"Not you, Danny Dickens!"

Danny stopped. Now what? Miss May was standing right by his desk and pointing at his sketch pad.

"This shouldn't be out during lesson time, Danny," she said. "You can't concentrate on what you are supposed to be doing if you're drawing pictures."

She flipped over a few pages of Danny's sketch pad. She knew Danny loved

drawing. Most of the pictures were funny –
dancing bananas, a cow in a hot air
balloon, a snail race. She stared at a picture
of a fuzzy-haired character with glasses and

a long nose. It looked strangely familiar. Danny had done pictures of all his teachers. This one of the Headmaster was one of his favourites.

Miss May smiled.

"Mmm! Not bad!" she said. "But not in school time, please."

Danny nodded.

"Okay. Sorry," he said. He picked up the sketch book before she found the picture of herself. "Can I go now?"

"Just one more thing," said Miss May.

She held out a white envelope. Danny's heart sank. It wasn't a letter asking his parents to a Parents' Evening, was it?

"They're too busy at the moment," he blurted out. "They've got Inspectors coming and loads to do and orange hair and stuff."

Miss May looked startled.

"It's for your grandfather," she said. "It's an invitation. I wondered if he would like to come into school and bring one of his new inventions. It's for our special 'How Things

Work' project."

Danny took the envelope. What a relief! It was only for Grandad. Miss May had heard all about Grandad's inventions. Danny had been telling everyone at school about them since he was in Year One. And he had been telling everyone about Grandad's latest invention all term. Everyone was expecting it to be something amazing.

"Could he bring it in?" said Miss May.

Danny nodded.

"I hope so!" he said. "He did say it would be ready now!"

Danny only lived around the corner from school. He was allowed to walk home on his own. Today he ran. He was home in three minutes. He rushed straight to the workshop.

"Slow down there!" said Grandad as Danny burst through the door and tossed his school stuff to one side.

Danny was about to say, "Where is it? Let's see it, then!", but he didn't need to.

There in front of him, after all that waiting, was Grandad's latest invention. It was amazing! Fantastic! Danny had never seen anything like it.

"What is it?"

Grandad was carefully tightening a few last screws.

"It's a Remote-Controlled Room Tidier!" he said.

"Wow!"

"Possibly the first in the world!"

"Wow!"

"It can be used in any room in the house!"

"Cool!"

"Want to see it in action?"

Danny nodded.

Grandad picked up a newspaper and placed it next to his Room Robot. Danny thought it looked a bit like a robot with a flat head. Grandad twiddled with the remote control. An arm reached out from the robot and grabbed the newspaper. It placed it on its flat head. The arm went down. Grandad made the robot move forwards and then to the left. He pressed a red button on the control and the top of the robot flipped forwards shooting the newspaper across the workshop. It landed neatly in the waste paper bin by the door.

"Wow! It really works, Grandad!"

Grandad looked pleased. "Of course it works! Want to have a go?"

Danny certainly did. The two of them spent the next hour tidying the workshop. Danny liked shooting objects across the room back on to shelves or into boxes. Breakable things were carried carefully across the room by the robot arm and placed gently down. In no time at all Grandad's workshop was looking more organised than it had ever done before. It was fantastic! Everyone at school was going to love it.

Danny told Grandad about Miss May's invitation and gave him the letter.

"Will you take the robot?" he asked.

"I don't see why not!" said Grandad. "We could walk it to school. Maybe get it to do a bit of tidying up in your classroom."

Grandad moved the robot in towards a mug of cold coffee. It carried the cup across the workshop. Then, to their horror, it did something it hadn't done before. The arm jerked and started swinging backwards and forwards. Before Grandad could stop it, it had flung the cold liquid all over itself. There was a horrible hissing sound and the Room Robot came to a sudden halt.

"Whoops!" said Grandad.

"It's broken!" Danny wailed. "Now we can't show anyone."

"It can be fixed," said Grandad.

"Won't you have to take it apart again?"

"Probably," said Grandad.

Danny groaned. The robot wouldn't be ready in time for Miss May's lesson.

Grandad hadn't got round to fixing the Breakfast Server yet so they couldn't take that. They couldn't have bits of toast flying around the classroom.

"How about the Automatic Back Scratcher?" said Grandad.

Danny had forgotten about that one. It would have to do. But it couldn't be as much fun as the robot, could it?

Chapter Three

If anyone had told Danny what was going to happen next, he would never have believed it.

There he was the next morning all ready to go to school with Grandad's Automatic Back Scratcher in its box when a terrible commotion came from the bathroom.

It was Grandad.

"What is it, Grandad?" said Lily and Mum.

"What's up, Grandad?" said Danny and Dad.

Grandad, dressed and ready to set off to school with Danny and the invention, was looking very worried.

"It'sh my new falsh teeth!" he said. "I only put them down for a moment. I must have knocked them."

Mum gasped.

"You don't mean…" she said.

Grandad nodded.

"I'm afraid sho!" he said. " 'hey've 'allen in the 'oilet. Gone! Flushed avay."

Danny realised this was terrible for two reasons. First of all, they would have to get the plumber out. The plumber would have to dismantle the pipe and fish around in the U-bend looking for Grandad's teeth. Secondly, Grandad would never go to school without his smart new set of teeth and talking funny and it was already time to leave.

"You'll just 'ave to go w'out me, Danny!" said Grandad.

"But what about the 'How Things Work' project?" said Danny.

"You'll just have to show everyone how it works," said Mum. "You can do that, can't you Danny? I'm sure Miss May won't mind."

Danny wasn't sure about that. It wouldn't be the same without Grandad to explain things. Everyone would be so disappointed. What would Miss May say?

Danny felt very nervous.

He prayed before he set off. "Help me to know what to say. And please don't let anyone ask any awkward questions."

It was soon time for the lesson.

"Danny's grandad can't be here to show us his invention himself," said Miss May.

"Ohh!" said everyone.

"His teeth fell in the toilet this morning," she went on.

Everyone burst out laughing.

But Miss May didn't laugh.

"But," she added, "Danny has brought something in to show us instead."

"Ooh!" said everyone.

Danny carefully took the Automatic Back Scratcher out of the cardboard box. He had to place it on his head. He carefully strapped it in place. Then he pressed the ON switch on one side of it. Everyone cheered and laughed as the scratching arm at the back reached down and moved backwards and forwards tickling and scratching Danny's back.

"It's a wonderful invention!" said Miss May. "It's very clever. Can you show us how it works, Danny?"

Danny swallowed. This was the bit he had been dreading.

Danny removed the gadget from his head and took some of it apart. He tried to remember what Grandad had said about how the different bits were connected and what made them move. He showed them where the battery was.

"Fascinating!" said Miss May. "I think it's wonderful. Your grandad has got a real gift for inventing things. Put it back together, Danny and then perhaps someone would like to try it out. Any volunteers?"

"Coo-ee, Miss May!"

"Can I have a go?"

"Can I go third?"

Everyone was waving their arms about. Everyone wanted to try out the Automatic Back Scratcher. Miss May decided they would all take turns, but *she* would go first.

The whole class giggled as Danny fitted the gadget on to Miss May's head. Danny looked at it for a moment. Mmm. It didn't look quite right. Had he put it back together properly?

But it was too late. Miss May pressed the ON switch. The scratching arm started to swivel about, but it didn't reach down to give Miss May's back a good scratch. This time it swivelled round to the front and waved about wildly.

"Aghh!" said Miss May. "What's it doing?"

"I don't know," said Danny. "It's never done that before."

"Aghh!" cried Miss May again.

Everyone was laughing. The scratching arm had landed on her nose.

"Danny! Turn this thing off at once!"

Year Four were in fits of laughter.

"Wow!" cried Robert Belch. "Look at that! You've turned it into an automatic nose picker, Danny!"

When he got home from school that day Danny could still hear the sound of everyone laughing.

Grandad was in the workshop. His teeth had been rescued from the toilet. They had been specially cleaned and Grandad was glad to have them back. Danny told him what had happened at school.

"Sorry, Grandad," he said. "Have I broken it?"

Grandad chuckled.

"No!" he said. "I'll soon sort it out. I wish I could have seen the Automatic Nose Picker!"

"Hmm!" said Danny.

He went up to his room and flopped down on his bed. Then he did what he always did when he felt cross or upset. He got out his sketch book and started doodling. He did quite a good picture of Miss May wearing an automatic nose picker. It almost made him smile.

Then he talked to Jesus.

"Everyone is good at something." he prayed. "But why don't I seem to be good at anything?"

Then Dad put his head around the door.

"Doing your homework already?"

Danny shook his head. He told Dad what had happened at school. Dad sat down on the bed next to Danny.

"Never mind," he said. "Grandad will soon have it fixed. Don't worry. Anyway, it was Grandad's invention. He should have been the one to show everyone how it worked. That's what *he's* good at."

"That's just it," said Danny miserably. "Why is it that everyone in this family is good at something except me?"

"Well, that's just not true," said Dad. "God gives everyone something to be good at. We're all special to him."

Danny shook his head.

"It doesn't make sense."

"One day it will," said Dad. "One day you'll realise that God has given you something special to be good at too. And in the meantime you're pretty good at just being you. How about helping out downstairs?"

"The inspectors' visit?" said Danny.

Dad nodded.

"Exactly! It's tomorrow, remember."

Downstairs in the restaurant the family were getting things ready for the inspectors' visit. Lily was practising folding napkins into lily shapes. Mum was in the office throwing stuff out of a cupboard.

"We don't need these anymore," she said, tossing out an old pair of wellington boots. "Or this, or this, or this!"

Danny ducked as unwanted items flew towards him. There was a headless doll, a handleless bag, half an umbrella and a pair of old socks.

Mum kept some strange things in her office cupboard. Good idea to get rid of them before the inspectors came, thought Danny.

"I don't know what this is doing in here," said Mum, holding up an inflatable dinosaur. "Ah, at last, here are the papers I was looking for."

"I can help if you like," said Danny.

Mum passed Danny a bundle of old

magazines and catalogues to sort out.

"Just throw out all the old ones," she said.

Danny sorted the papers into three piles: Rubbish, Complete Rubbish and Keep For a Bit Longer. Only two things were in his Keep For a Bit Longer pile. One was a magazine that had a photograph of a chef throwing a bowl of jelly over another chef. The other was a leaflet which had YUMMY PUDDING COMPETITION in big letters on the front. Danny thought that sounded good. He looked inside. It had been sent by the restaurant inspectors.

"Is your restaurant due to have a visit from the restaurant inspectors?" the writing said. *"Then why not take part in our* YUMMY PUDDING COMPETITION? *Present your home-made original yummy pudding to the inspectors during their visit, and you could win one of our special award plaques to go on your restaurant wall."*

There was a photograph of one of the plaques.

YUMMY PUDDING AWARD
SPECIAL PRIZE – WITH HONOURS.

Danny thought one of those would look good on the wall of The Cuckoo Lane Restaurant.

He showed Mum the leaflet.

"Dad's brilliant at making puddings," he said. "He could easily win!"

Mum laughed.

Danny was right. Dad had invented all sorts of super puddings. There was his Chocolate Doughnut Delight, the Tingling Toffee with extra cream and the Pink and Purple Puffs. Any one of those was a winner. Or maybe Dad could think of an even more mouth-watering surprise. After all, he was a super chef.

Danny ran off towards the kitchen clutching the leaflet.

"I'm going to show Dad," he said. He wanted to persuade Dad to enter the competition.

Chapter Four

Dad and Lily were in the restaurant.

At first Dad wasn't sure about entering the Yummy Pudding Competition. He had a lot of things to do, he said.

Lily had finished folding the napkins into lily shapes. She had placed them all carefully on a tray ready for the next day.

"Oh, go on, Dad," she said. "Danny's right. You should enter one of your puddings. You'll win a plaque. We might get photographed for the newspaper."

"We might be on the telly!" said Danny. "We might be famous!"

Imagine what everyone at school would say when they found out that Danny Dickens lived at a famous, award-winning pudding restaurant.

"You deserve to win," Lily added.

Dad laughed. "A chef's best award is watching people eat what you've just cooked!" he said.

"Well, even more people will want to come and eat here if we win," said Lily.

Dad thought about that. He decided Danny and Lily were right.

"I suppose I could make something in time," he agreed. "It will be fun having a go – even if we don't win. I've got a lot more sorting out to do first, though."

"I'll help!" said Danny. Then he had an idea.

He dashed down to the workshop where Grandad had been working on his Room Robot.

"Is it ready, Grandad?" Danny asked.

"It certainly is!" said Grandad.

"Can we test it out in the restaurant?"

said Danny. "Dad's got loads of tidying up to do for the inspectors' visit tomorrow. When he's done that, he's going to make a pudding for the Yummy Pudding Competition. If he wins a prize we'll get a special certificate to go on the restaurant wall and we might get our pictures in the newspaper."

Grandad was very impressed and he was pleased that his new invention was going to come in useful so soon.

Dad and Mum and Lily were amazed when they saw the Room Robot.

"Extraordinary!" said Dad.

"Fantastic!" said Mum.

"Does it work?" said Lily.

"Does it work!" laughed Grandad. "Of course! Let's give them a demonstration, Danny!"

Grandad and Danny showed everyone how the robot could collect up all the dirty tablecloths and put them in a pile, throw rubbish into the bins and even carry a tray of mustard pots into the restaurant kitchen for refilling and then carry them back again.

Everyone was very impressed. With Grandad's new invention to help, everything would be ready for the next day in no time. Dad would have plenty of time for making one of his yummiest puddings. At least, that's what everyone thought, until...

"Catch, Lily!" Danny called. He was clearing the dessert trolley and placed a bunch of cherries on the robot. Swish! The cherries flew threw the air towards Lily. Lily missed and the cherries splattered all over the floor.

"Oops!" said Danny. "Sorry!"

Just at that moment Dad entered the room with an armful of bread baskets. He was holding so many that he couldn't see over the top of them.

"Look out, Dad!" cried Danny.

"Aggghhh!" cried Dad.

"Oh no!" cried Danny.

"Oh, Dad!" cried Lily.

"Mind the bread baskets!" cried Mum.

"Too late!" cried Grandad, as Dad stepped straight on to the cherries. Squish! Then he skidded sideways. Squelch! He lost his balance and landed with a crash.

They all rushed to help him up. Dad sat up. He crawled on to his hands and knees.

Then he stopped.

"Aghh!"

"What's the matter?" cried Mum. "Have you broken something?

"No!" said Dad. "It's my back. It's gone funny again. I can't stand up!"

This was terrible. The last time Dad's back had gone 'funny' he couldn't stand up for two days. He had to crawl around on his hands and knees. The customers had thought it was very strange. The restaurant inspectors were also going to think it was very strange.

"Oh no!" said Mum. "You'd better go and lie down. Let's hope it's better by the morning."

Dad crawled slowly towards the door. It didn't look as though he would be better by the morning.

Danny looked glum.

"It's all my fault," he said. "I should have left the cherries."

"No," said Dad. He squelched through the squashed cherries. "I should have looked where I was going. Anyway, the cherries were going off. We can't have bad fruit on the dessert trolley when the inspectors arrive."

Chapter Five

Danny decided to go to bed early. It seemed the best thing to do when you were having a bad day. But he couldn't get to sleep. It felt like everything was his fault. What if Dad still couldn't stand up in the morning? What if he had to spend the whole day crawling about on his hands and knees? And worst of all – how could he make the yummy pudding for the Yummy Pudding Competition?

Danny sat up. He felt miserable. He picked up his sketch book. But he couldn't think of anything to draw.

"Please let everything be okay

tomorrow," he prayed. Danny knew Jesus always listened when he talked to him.

Danny lay down again. He tried hard but he still couldn't sleep. He was still awake when the grown-ups went to bed. He put the lamp on. Then he reached for his sketch pad and pencil again. He drew a picture of Grandad's robot. It was very good. He put the sketch pad down again. He still didn't feel sleepy.

Danny decided to get up. He would go down to the kitchen and get a glass of cola. Then he would feel better. Then maybe he would sleep.

Danny crept quietly along the corridor towards the kitchen. The floorboards creaked a bit, but the only other sound was Dad's snoring.

Then, when he was still sitting at the kitchen table with his drink, he heard it – another sound. Not floorboards, not snoring. More of a sneaking, creeping sort of sound. Danny's heart pounded. Then he heard quiet voices. They weren't the voices of anyone he recognised. Danny gasped, jumped up and hid behind the kitchen door. Burglars! It must be burglars!

Danny stayed where he was and kept very still. What should he do? The voices appeared to be coming from the sitting room. He would have to creep back to his parents' room. His mum kept her mobile phone by the bed. She could call the police.

Very bravely, Danny walked as slowly and

silently as he could along the corridor. He was almost there when something strange happened to the voices coming from the sitting room. They weren't talking anymore – *they were singing!*

I don't believe it! Danny said to himself. How could I have been so daft!

He marched back to the sitting room and pushed the door open. The TV was on and slumped in his favourite armchair was – not a burglar – Grandad! He'd nodded off. Danny gave him a nudge.

Grandad jumped and held up his arms.

"Take anything!" he cried. "But not the TV!"

"Grandad!" Danny said. "It's me, Danny!"

Grandad put his arms down.

"Well, what are *you* doing up at this time?" he asked.

"Well, what are *you* doing up at this time?" replied Danny.

Grandad hauled himself out of the chair and switched off the TV.

"Couldn't sleep," he said.

"Me neither," said Danny. "I got up to get a glass of cola. Do you want one?"

Grandad didn't fancy that. Fizzy drinks always gave him burps. Sometimes hiccups as well. He'd have a mug of hot tomato soup instead.

Danny was glad Grandad had got up as well. It was nice to have someone to talk to. Grandad knew how bad Danny felt about tripping Dad up. But it was just an accident. Dad would be fine again soon, he said. Danny started to feel a bit better. Then he had an idea.

"I suppose we could have a go at making one of those yummy puddings for the competition ourselves," he said. "Wouldn't Dad be surprised?"

"That's a brilliant idea!" said Grandad.

"The trouble is," said Danny, "we don't know any of Dad's special recipes. He keeps them all secret, doesn't he?"

Grandad tapped the side of his nose.

"Sshh!" he said. "Let's go down to the

restaurant kitchen and see what we can do!"

"What, now?" said Danny.

"There won't be any time in the morning," said Grandad. "Come on. And watch out for burglars!"

Chapter Six

Down in the restaurant kitchen, Grandad looked in the fridge and freezers and Danny raided the ingredients cupboard. They were looking for clues. Neither of them knew what secret ingredients Dad put into his yummy puddings. They were going to have to guess.

"There's half a Chocolate Delight left in the fridge," said Grandad. "We could make one of those."

Danny shook his head.

"There's no chocolate left in the cupboard," he said. "I think we should make something bright and cheerful looking."

"Of course," said Grandad. "In that case we should make one of his Strawberry Surprises."

Everyone loved Dad's Strawberry Surprise. It was made of crushed chocolate biscuits and a creamy strawberry filling, and was decorated with real strawberries and different coloured hundreds and thousands. That would be easy to make. But then there was the difficult bit. No one knew what the secret ingredient was that Dad always added to the creamy strawberry filling.

"Maybe it's custard," said Danny.

"No. It's a stronger taste than that," said Grandad.

Danny looked along the row of spice bottles in the ingredients cupboard.

"What about ginger?"

"We'll try ginger!" Grandad agreed.

It took Grandad and Danny ten minutes to get all the ingredients together. Then Danny set up the food whisk.

"Are you sure you know what you're

54

doing with that, Danny?" said Grandad.

"No problem!" said Danny. He stuck the end of the electric whisk into the bowl of fresh cream. He turned the switch to ON. The whisk whirred into action at top speed. Cream splattered everywhere. A lump of it shot upwards and splashed onto

Danny's forehead. Danny wiped it off with his hand.

Then he looked for the chocolate biscuits. He needed a whole packet to crush into crumbs.

"I can only find jammie dodgers," said Danny. "Do you think they'll do instead?"

Grandad thought jammie dodgers would do nicely. They crushed them up and tipped the crumbs into the bottom of the dessert dish.

"It looks a bit gooey," said Danny.

"We'll call it Strawberry Gooey Surprise then," said Grandad. "Now let's tip this creamy mixture on the top."

They started pouring the creamy mixture on top of the crunchy base. For some reason it had gone a bit lumpy.

"It doesn't look right," said Danny. He dipped his finger into the mixture and tasted it. "It's got a cheesy taste."

Grandad tried some.

"Mmm! Very nice though!" he said. "Maybe I whisked up some cottage cheese instead of cream!"

"Oh no!"

"It doesn't matter," said Grandad. "It still tastes good. We'll call it Strawberry Gooey Lumpy Surprise."

Danny was a bit worried about that name. But Grandad was good at inventing things. Now for the pinch of ginger.

"We should have put it in the cream mixture," said Grandad. "Never mind. Just sprinkle it over the top. Give it a good shake."

Danny gave the ginger container a good shake and tipped it upside down over the pudding. Plop! The top fell off and a lump of very strong ginger powder landed in the bowl.

"I've ruined it!" Danny wailed. "That will make it taste awful!"

"Nonsense," said Grandad. "The inspectors don't have to eat that bit. A lump of ginger in the middle makes it much more interesting."

They both arranged the slices of

strawberries on the top of the pudding. Then they sprinkled on the hundreds and thousands. Danny got a bit carried away. It was more like millions and billions. It was definitely an original recipe. But would it be as good as one of Dad's? Would it be good

enough to win the Yummy Pudding Competition?

Chapter Seven

Even Dad's snoring didn't stop Danny falling asleep after that. By the time he and Grandad had cleaned up and washed up after their pudding making, it was half-past twelve. Danny fell asleep as soon as his head touched the pillow. The next morning he was last to wake up.

For a few moments he lay there feeling cosy and still half asleep. Gradually Danny's brain started to wake up. First of all, he remembered that the teachers were having a special meeting day. Great! An extra day off! Then he remembered it was the day the restaurant inspectors were coming. He remembered Dad's back. Danny jumped and sat up.

"Oh no!" he groaned out loud.

Then he thought about the pudding he and Grandad had made the night before.

"Oh yes!"

Danny sprang out of bed. He put his right foot into his left slipper then he pulled a jumper over the top of his pyjamas. He had to get up to see how Dad was. He had to tell Dad about the pudding he and Grandad had made the night before. Dad would be so surprised. He put his left foot into his right slipper and hurried out of his room.

The flat was strangely quiet. Danny put his head around the kitchen door. There was no one there. Then he realised. Of course, everyone must be downstairs in the restaurant. With such an important and busy day ahead they would have to make an early start.

Danny leaped down the stairs two at a time and burst into the restaurant kitchen.

He was right. Grandad and Lily were already hard at work polishing the cutlery and Mum was checking the menus with Dad. Dad was no longer on his hands and knees.

"Are you better, Dad?" Danny asked. "Can you stand up properly yet?"

Dad rubbed his back. He was standing in a sort of ape-like position with his arms dangling forwards around his knees.

"Getting better all the time, Danny, thank you," he said. "Can't really stand up right yet but it's certainly better. At least I'll be able to meet the inspectors."

Danny tried to imagine Dad meeting the inspectors. Well, maybe they would be too busy wondering why his parents had carrot coloured hair to wonder why one of them couldn't stand upright.

"Don't worry, Dad," said Lily. "Mum and I are going to do most of the work in the kitchen today."

"Yes," said Mum, "we'll have to forget about that pudding contest as well. Sorry, Danny. Maybe next year."

Danny looked at Grandad. Grandad looked at Danny.

"Ah," he said. "Well, that's where you're wrong. Danny, show them the surprise!"

"Surprise!" said Dad. "What surprise?"

Danny went over to the fridge and took out the Strawberry Surprise.

"That's fantastic!" said Lily.

"That's wonderful!" said Mum.

"That's a Yummy Pudding winner!" laughed Dad.

Grandad explained how Danny had felt sorry about tripping him up, even though it was really an accident, and how they hadn't wanted the restaurant to miss out on entering the contest.

"It's brilliant!" said Dad. "If it tastes as good as it looks it's bound to win a prize. Well done, Danny!"

Danny placed the pudding carefully back in the fridge.

"Do you think it will taste okay, Grandad?" he said. "The recipe wasn't the same as Dad's, was it?"

"It's supposed to be original," said Grandad.

"That's right," said Mum. "It's in the competition rules. The pudding has to be original."

"That's okay then!" said Danny. Then he thought, as long as no one tastes that lump of ginger in the middle. Maybe they should have a jug of cold water ready in case.

"You've got your feet on the wrong legs again," said Grandad.

Danny looked down at his slippers. He swapped them over so that they were on the right feet.

"You'd better go and get dressed properly, Danny," said Mum.

Danny leaped upstairs again. He was dressed in no time. Then he sat down on his bed and opened his sketch pad. He drew the Strawberry Surprise. Then he drew a medal next to it. He wrote five words on the medal. YUMMY PUDDING AWARD. FIRST PRIZE.

He went back down to the restaurant and showed everyone his picture. But Dad was too busy to look.

"Leave it in Mum's office," he said. "I'll look later."

A low rumbling sound was coming from Danny's stomach. He was definitely ready for breakfast.

Chapter Eight

Back in the flat Danny helped himself to a bowl of Coco Pops followed by a chocolate spread sandwich. He filled the bowl with so much cereal that when he put the milk on, it overflowed.

"Scrumptious!" said Danny, tucking in. "An excellent start to a no-school day."

He was just finishing off the last mouthful of chocolate sandwich when Grandad came into the kitchen.

"It's five to ten already," said Grandad. "The inspectors will be here any minute. You and I have got to keep out of the way."

"Ohh!" Danny sighed. "Can't I at least see what they look like?"

"Of course," said Grandad, "but we must keep out of the way while they are doing their job."

At ten o'clock there was a ring on the restaurant doorbell. Danny ran to the top of the stairs and looked down. Mum opened the door and said good morning. A man and a woman stood there.

"Good morning," said the man. "I'm Mr Peeky and this is Miss Plum. We've come to inspect your restaurant."

"Nice to meet you," said Mum. "Come on in. I'm Mrs Dickens. This is Mr Dickens and this is our daughter, Lily Dickens."

Everyone shook hands. Miss Plum was very round. Mr Peeky was very thin. He was looking a bit pale. Danny wondered if it was the shock of seeing the orange hair.

"I'm afraid I'm not very good at travelling on long journeys," he said. "I always get travel sick."

"How terrible!" said Mum. "Come
through to the office and have a sit down
and a cup of tea."

"That would be nice," said Mr Peeky.
"Thank you very much."

Grandad and Danny went back into the kitchen. Danny looked at the clock. They washed up. Danny looked at the clock again. Grandad read the newspaper and Danny looked at a comic. Then he looked at the clock again. It was boring being upstairs. He wanted to know what was going on down in the restaurant. Were the inspectors in the office? Had they finished their tea? Was Mr Peeky feeling better yet?

"I'm bored!" said Danny tossing the comic down. "I wish we could do something."

Grandad put the newspaper down.

"What we've got to do is make ourselves useful," he said. "And I've got the perfect idea."

Danny didn't often wish Grandad hadn't had one of his ideas, but right then he did.

"Cleaning?" said Danny as Grandad hauled the vacuum cleaner out of the cleaning cupboard.

"Of course!" said Grandad. "It will make

the time whizz by!"

Danny started in the lounge. Grandad moved the rug and cushions so he could clean underneath.

"This cleaner is very powerful, isn't it, Grandad?" said Danny as Grandad struggled to pull Mum's favourite cushion back out of the suction tube.

"It certainly is," said Grandad.

"I don't suppose you've ever thought of inventing a vacuum cleaner that works on its own?" said Danny. He had to shout above the noise of the cleaner.

Grandad said he might do that one day.

Danny went all round the lounge and then the bedrooms and then the landing and stairs. He was almost down to the bottom step with the cleaning nozzle. He could just about reach with the vacuum cleaner balanced dangerously on a step half-way down.

He was concentrating too hard to notice the office door open and Mum appear with Miss Plum and Mr Peeky. The next thing he knew there was a crash and the cleaner bounced and banged down to the bottom of the stairs. Danny jumped out of the way, swinging the cleaning nozzle around. There was a nasty slurping, guzzling noise and something very strange happened to Miss Plum. Danny dropped the cleaning nozzle.

Mum, Dad, Mr Peeky, Grandad and Danny all stared at Miss Plum in disbelief.

"Oh!" said Mum and Mr Peeky at the same time.

"Wow!" said Danny.

"Whoops!" said Grandad, who was standing at the top of the stairs.

The hoover was still making that horrible slurping, guzzling sound.

"Well, what are you all staring at?" said Miss Plum.

"I'm so sorry, Miss Plum," said Mum. She stepped forward and switched off the vacuum cleaner. "This is my son, Danny. I think he was just trying to do something useful."

It was then that Miss Plum saw what the problem was. Not Danny, not Grandad but the blonde hairy thing that was sticking out of the end of the vacuum cleaner nozzle.

She clutched her head. It was a bit grey, Danny thought, but not quite as bald as Grandad's.

"My hair!" she shrieked. "What's happened to my hair?"

"The vacuum cleaner has started to suck it up!" said Mum.

"What's happened to it? What's happened to it?" Miss Plum shrieked again.

Danny was trying hard not to laugh. So Miss Plum had been wearing a wig!

"Sshh!" said Mum. She knelt down and tried to pull the wig out of the cleaner.

"Gently! Gently!" said Miss Plum.

"It seems to be stuck," said Mum.

"Let me have a go," Mr Peeky offered.

Gripping the hair piece, he tugged hard. There was a ripping sound and the wig was free.

"It's ruined!" cried Miss Plum. "There's a bit missing and there's dirt all over it."

"Don't worry," said Mum. "I'll give it a quick wash. If we comb it carefully you won't notice the missing bit. I'm very good with hair."

Miss Plum looked at Mum's orange hair.

"I think I need some more tea," she said.

Chapter Nine

After two more cups of strong tea, Miss Plum felt much better. Lily offered her a plate of Dad's home-made biscuits. Mum soon had the hair sorted out.

Miss Plum arranged her newly washed and combed wig on her head and the restaurant inspection continued.

Danny and Grandad had put the vacuum cleaner away. While Grandad had gone back to reading his newspaper, Danny had crept back downstairs to see what was happening. He would keep out of the way. After all, it wasn't as if he was going to cause any more disasters, was it?

The inspectors found the kitchen clean and tidy. The restaurant was due to open at lunch time and Dad and Lily were busy preparing vegetables and salads.

Grandad's Room Robot had been left in the corner of the kitchen. Miss Plum looked at it suspiciously. She held on to her hair as she walked past.

The inspectors inspected the fridges and freezers. They looked in the cupboards and on the shelves. They examined the menus. By the time they moved on to the restaurant it was nearly lunch time. Lily opened the main door. There were already two customers waiting. She showed them to a table while the inspectors were still looking around.

The smell of food was starting to fill the air.

"Hmm!" said Mr Peeky looking at the plain white walls. "Very clean. Excellent. A bit bare though."

"A few pictures of food would look nice," said Miss Plum. "That delicious smell coming from the kitchen is making me feel very hungry. Shall we stay for lunch, Mr Peeky?"

Mr Peeky agreed that it would be a good idea to stay for lunch. It was getting rather late. Lily showed them to a table and gave them a menu each.

"Mmm," said Mr Peeky. "I think I'll have a lettuce and tomato sandwich and a glass of water. Thank you."

"Mmm," said Miss Plum, "I'll have two large bowls of tomato soup, spaghetti bolognese with cheese and extra cheese, apple pie, cheese and biscuits and three cups of coffee."

"Very well," said Lily.

A few minutes later another six people entered the restaurant. Not long after that, even more customers arrived. The restaurant was very busy. Dad asked Danny to fetch Grandad. They needed extra help in the kitchen.

"Can't I help?" said Danny.

Dad shook his head.

"You're too young," he said. "I don't think the inspectors would approve."

So Danny stayed where he was, watching in the doorway. The restaurant hadn't been as busy as this for weeks. The inspectors would be very impressed, thought Danny.

"Everyone wants soup today," said Lily walking past with a trayful of soup bowls.

"Don't forget the bread rolls!" said Mum.

"I'll have to come back for them," said Lily.

It wasn't fair. Danny wished Dad would let him help. He could carry the bread rolls. He looked at Grandad's Room Robot and had an idea.

"Why don't we use the Room Robot, Grandad?" he said.

Grandad had been carefully taking plates out of the plate warmer.

"That's a good idea!" he said.

Dad thought it was a good idea, too. It would speed things up a bit.

They soon had the robot running

backwards and forwards from the kitchen to the restaurant. The customers thought it was brilliant. The inspectors thought it was brilliant. Soon everyone had their soup and bread rolls.

"I could never have got round everyone that fast!" said Lily.

Mum and Dad were pleased with the way the inspection was going. So far Mr Peeky and Miss Plum had liked The Cuckoo Lane Restaurant. They thought all the paperwork was in order. They thought the kitchen was clean and tidy. And now they were starting to discover how fantastic the food was too.

Then Danny remembered something. What about the Yummy Pudding Competition? Everyone had been so busy they had forgotten about it. Danny had an idea. What if he got the Strawberry Surprise ready? He could place it on the robot ready to be sent in to the inspectors.

No one noticed Danny sneak into the kitchen and take the Strawberry Surprise out of the fridge. No one noticed him put it on the robot. No one noticed him pick up the remote control.

Danny waited for the right moment. Then as soon as Mr Peeky had finished his sandwiches and Miss Plum had finished her first bowl of soup, he sent in the Yummy Pudding.

"Ooh! Look at that!" said one of the customers.

"That looks delicious!" said another.

Danny carefully controlled the robot as it made its way over to the inspectors. Any minute now they would get such a surprise!

"Oh no!" Danny wiggled the controls. "Something's wrong with the remote control!"

Grandad stopped what he was doing and looked at Danny.

"What are you doing?"

"I'm sending in the Yummy Pudding!" said Danny. "It was working okay but something's gone wrong. I can't get it to slow down and stop."

The robot was whizzing up to the inspectors' table.

"Look out!" cried one of the customers. "There's a runaway pudding!"

Miss Plum saw it next.

"Help!" she gasped.

Grandad leapt as fast as he could towards the robot.

"Switch it off! Switch it off!" said Lily.

"I can't!" said Danny. "It's stuck. Oh no, now what's it doing?"

The robot had crashed into Mr Peeky's chair. The bump made the pudding slide towards the edge of the tray. Grandad flew towards it. Then just as Danny was thinking things couldn't get any worse...

Suddenly the robot catapulted the pudding upwards above the inspectors' table. Thinking quickly Grandad ran towards it with his arms ready to catch it. As it landed he caught his foot on one of the robot wheels and fell on to the table, straight into Miss Plum's soup bowl. The pudding landed neatly in Miss Plum's lap.

"Oh!" cried Mr Peeky.

"Help!" cried Miss Plum.

"Oh no!" cried the customers.

"There's pudding all over me!" cried Miss

Plum. "And someone in my soup."

"Missed it!" said Grandad, removing himself from the soup bowl.

Mum, Dad, Lily and Danny and some of the customers rushed towards the inspectors' table.

"That was our entry for the Yummy

Pudding Competition!" said Danny, pointing to the pink and red and creamy gooey mess in Miss Plum's lap. "It's called Strawberry Surprise!"

Chapter Ten

After all the excitement Danny was glad it was a normal school day again the next day. He had been disappointed about the Strawberry Surprise. Mr Peeky had run his finger around the bowl and tasted it. He said it was such a shame it had ended up in Miss Plum's lap.

Danny told everyone at school what had happened. They all laughed. Then Danny laughed. At break time he looked in his rucksack for his sketch pad. He wanted to sketch a picture of the pudding landing in Miss Plum's lap and Grandad flying through the air and landing in the soup.

Everyone could see how funny it had really been. But the sketch book wasn't there. He must have left it at home.

"Can you get your grandad to let us borrow the robot at school?" asked Robert. "We could get it to serve up the school dinners and have a pudding throwing contest."

After school Danny went straight to his room to look for his sketch pad. It wasn't in its usual place, under his bed.

He found Mum, Dad, Grandad and Lily in the kitchen having a drink. He was about to ask them about the sketch pad when Mum spoke first.

"Mr Peeky rang this afternoon," she said.

Danny held his breath.

"The restaurant passed the inspection!"

Danny gave Mum a hug. After all their hard work thank goodness everything had been all right.

"What about the Yummy Pudding Competition?" he said. "Did we win a prize?"

Dad shook his head.

"Never mind, Danny," he said. "It was a good try though. It looked delicious. We might have won a prize if it hadn't ended up in Miss Plum's lap."

Danny was disappointed. If only Dad had had time to make the pudding. They would have won then.

"Don't look sad, Danny," said Grandad. "You might not have won anything with your Strawberry Surprise but we've got another surprise for you. This way!"

"What sort of surprise?" said Danny. They all followed Grandad downstairs to the restaurant.

"Notice anything different?" said Lily.

Danny looked around the room.

"Mmm," said Danny, "There *is* something different. It's... it's... "

Danny stared in amazement. He could hardly believe his eyes. There on the restaurant walls hung his best sketches. Except they didn't look like just sketches any more. Someone had carefully framed

them in smart wooden picture frames and arranged them around the restaurant.

"It was Miss Plum's idea," said Dad. "She thought we needed some pictures. The walls looked too bare. She saw your sketch pad in the office. You must have left it there."

"And why go out and buy pictures when we've got our own talented artist in the family?" said Mum.

"They look brilliant!" said Danny. "Much better than when they were in the book."

"And now everyone can enjoy them," said Dad.

Mum liked Danny's dancing banana picture best. Dad liked the cow in the hot air balloon. Lily and Grandad liked the snail race. But Danny's favourite was the one of Miss May wearing the automatic nose picker.

"That's funny," said Grandad, "Mr Peeky said that was his favourite one too."

They all laughed.

"What did I tell you?" said Dad. "Everyone is good at something!"

Danny grinned. It was a nice feeling seeing his pictures on the wall.

Later, at bedtime, Mum came in to say goodnight. Danny was sitting up in bed with his sketch book.

"Don't stay up too long," she said.

"Okay," said Danny.

He wouldn't stay awake long. But first he

wanted to talk to God and thank him for sorting everything out. The restaurant had passed the inspection. Dad's back was much better – he was almost standing upright again. And the orange hair dye had nearly washed out – which was just as well, because Parents' Evening was only three days away now.

Secondly he wanted to start his next picture – the one of a Strawberry Surprise landing in Miss Plum's lap and Grandad falling in the soup.